April's Garden

Isla McGuckin   Catalina Echeverri

GRAFFEG

April was not happy.

Before they moved, Mamma had said,

"Every cloud has a silver lining.

4

This Book
belongs to:

_____

_____

For my daughters, Tallulah and Violet. I adore you.
Far more than words could ever express. I.McG.

For my three little flowers, Sofi, Abi and Violeta. C.E.

April's Garden
Published in Great Britain in 2023 by Graffeg Limited.

Written by Isla McGuckin copyright © 2023.
Illustrated by Catalina Echeverri copyright © 2023.
Designed and produced by Graffeg copyright © 2023.

Graffeg, 24 Stradey Park Business Centre,
Mwrwg Road, Llangennech, Llanelli,
Carmarthenshire, SA14 8YP, Wales, UK.
Tel: 01554 824000. www.graffeg.com.

Isla McGuckin and Catalina Echeverri are hereby
identified as the authors of this work in accordance with
section 77 of the Copyright, Designs and Patents Act
1988.

A CIP Catalogue record for this book is available from
the British Library.

The publisher acknowledges the financial support
of the Books Council of Wales. www.gwales.com.

ISBN 9781802583410

1 2 3 4 5 6 7 8 9

MIX
Paper from
responsible sources
FSC
www.fsc.org   FSC® C014138

We'll have our own room, in the new place.

It's big.

There's a garden."

5

Mamma was right
about the new place being big.

There were lots and lots of closed doors
with silent people behind them.

6

But there weren't any children, apart from April.

And the garden...

It was raining so much that

any clouds-with-silver-linings...

...were impossible to spot.

Mamma said,

"Draw the garden of your dreams.

The neighbourhood ladies brought paper and pens."

So, April drew.

Mamma said, smiling, "We'll save our pennies

for when we have a place of our own."

11

And then Mamma said,
"See what else is in those bags."
So, April looked.

There was a doll with tangled hair.

There were colouring books filled with somebody else's colouring.

And there was a set of cups that stacked.

April said, "For a baby!"

Mamma said,

"It's stopped
raining now.

Pop outside
for some
fresh air."

So, April did.

14

In the garden, there were puddles everywhere. April splashed a pebble into one of them.

She wondered what Mamma would say about getting a goldfish.

She could imagine what Mamma would say about getting a goldfish, "We'll save our pennies for when we have a place of our own." So, April decided not to ask.

It started to rain again. So, April went back inside.

Mamma said, "The neighbourhood ladies brought magazines, too.

And, look, some
of them have little
packets of seeds.

You could use those
cups as plant pots."

17

So, April ignored the rain and
ran back into the garden.

She scooped mud
into each cup.

18

She planted seeds that promised flowers in every size, shape and shade.

And then...

19

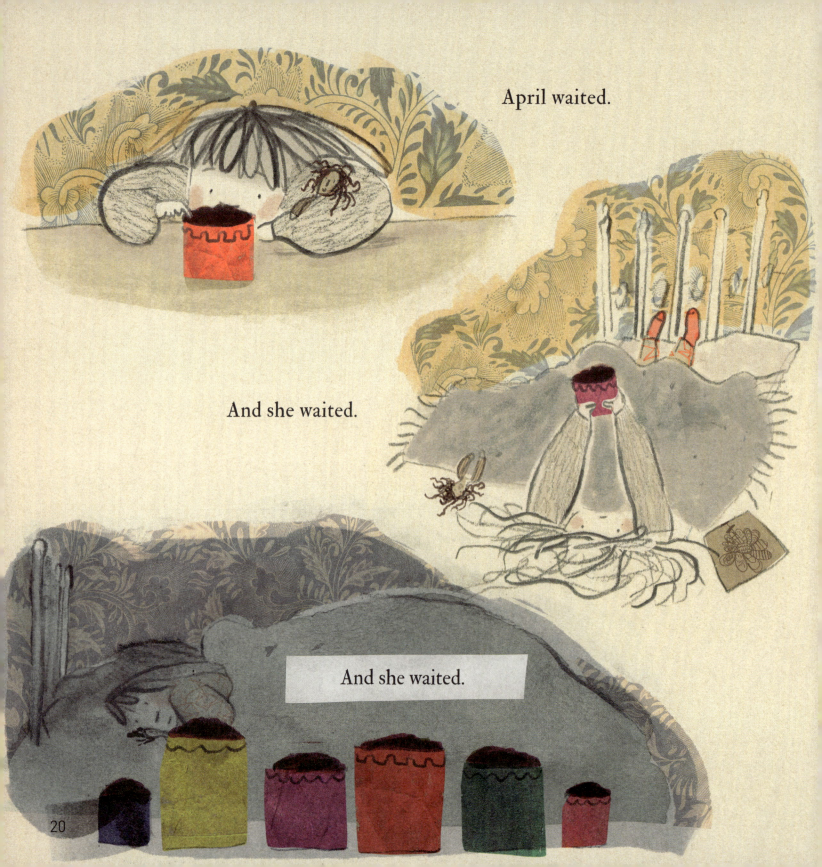

April waited.

And she waited.

And she waited.

20

Mamma said,
"Flowers take a while to grow.
Be patient, April."

So, April tried.

And she tried.

And she tried.

21

Mamma had once said,

"Hope is a lovely, magical sort of thinking.
It can help you to feel happy, no matter what."

But nothing felt hopeful or lovely or magical or happy.

So, April shouted, "I hate this place!"
And Mamma didn't say anything.
So, April ran outside.

Once, a very long time ago, Mamma had said, "Lovely things are just around the corner. Trust me. Please."

April wanted to know when the lovely things would stop being just around the corner.

She wanted something lovely now.

23

April felt cross.
She stamped her feet.
And she shouted up at the
rain-heavy clouds,

THiS iS noT Fair!

And then April felt
a little bit less cross.

The weeks passed.

And the months.

A day came for gathering up and moving on.

And, finally, Mamma said,

"This is home."

They had brought along the mud-filled cups.

Mamma said, "You need to find a good spot for them."

29

But April wasn't listening.

Because April had spotted something.

Tiny green shoots were
starting to unfurl in the
mud-filled cups.

Over the days and the
weeks that followed,
the tiny green shoots
became flowers in every
size, shape and shade.

And April was...

34

Happy.

Isla McGuckin

Isla McGuckin is a dreamer and a writer and the proud mother of daughters.

Endlessly optimistic, Isla believes that words have the power to open hearts, change minds and make the world a better place.

Born and raised in urban Yorkshire, Isla is now based in rural Donegal. Living in her tiny house beside the seaside – with her much-loved family of people and pets – feels like home.

Catalina Echeverri

Born in Bogotá, Colombia, Catalina Echeverri lives in London with her Northern Irish husband and their three daughters. Before settling in the UK, Catalina spent time in Italy, studying graphic design and eating pizza and ice cream every day that she could. When she'd eaten it all, she moved to Cambridge to study children's book illustration. She has worked in children's publishing ever since, illustrating more than 20 books in various countries. Catalina is never without her sketchbook and loves to draw inspiration from everyday life. She particularly enjoys working on projects that make a positive impact on people's lives. This is her first collaboration with Isla.